Young
Adult
741.5973
Houser

10-16-19
c.1

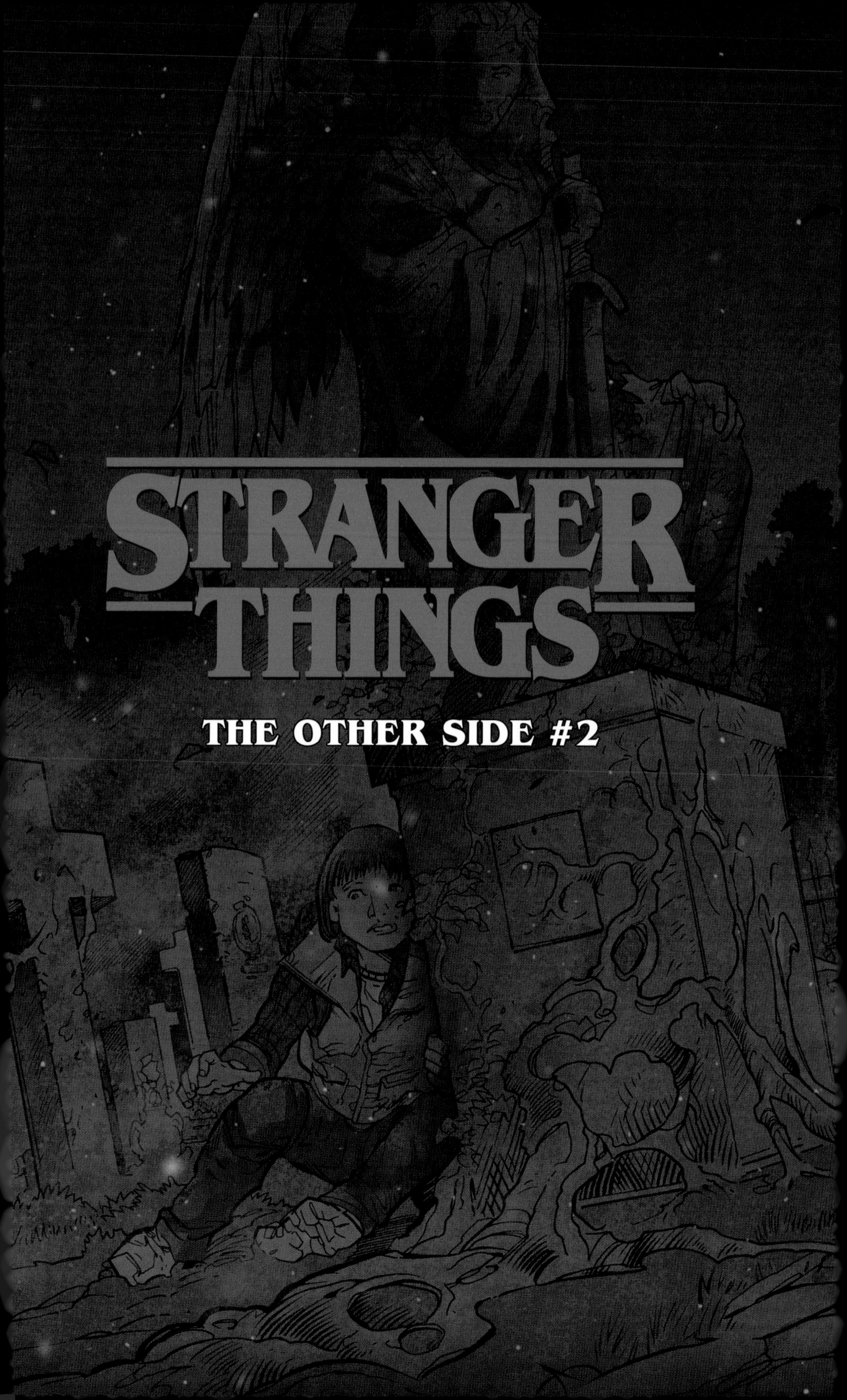
STRANGER THINGS
THE OTHER SIDE #2

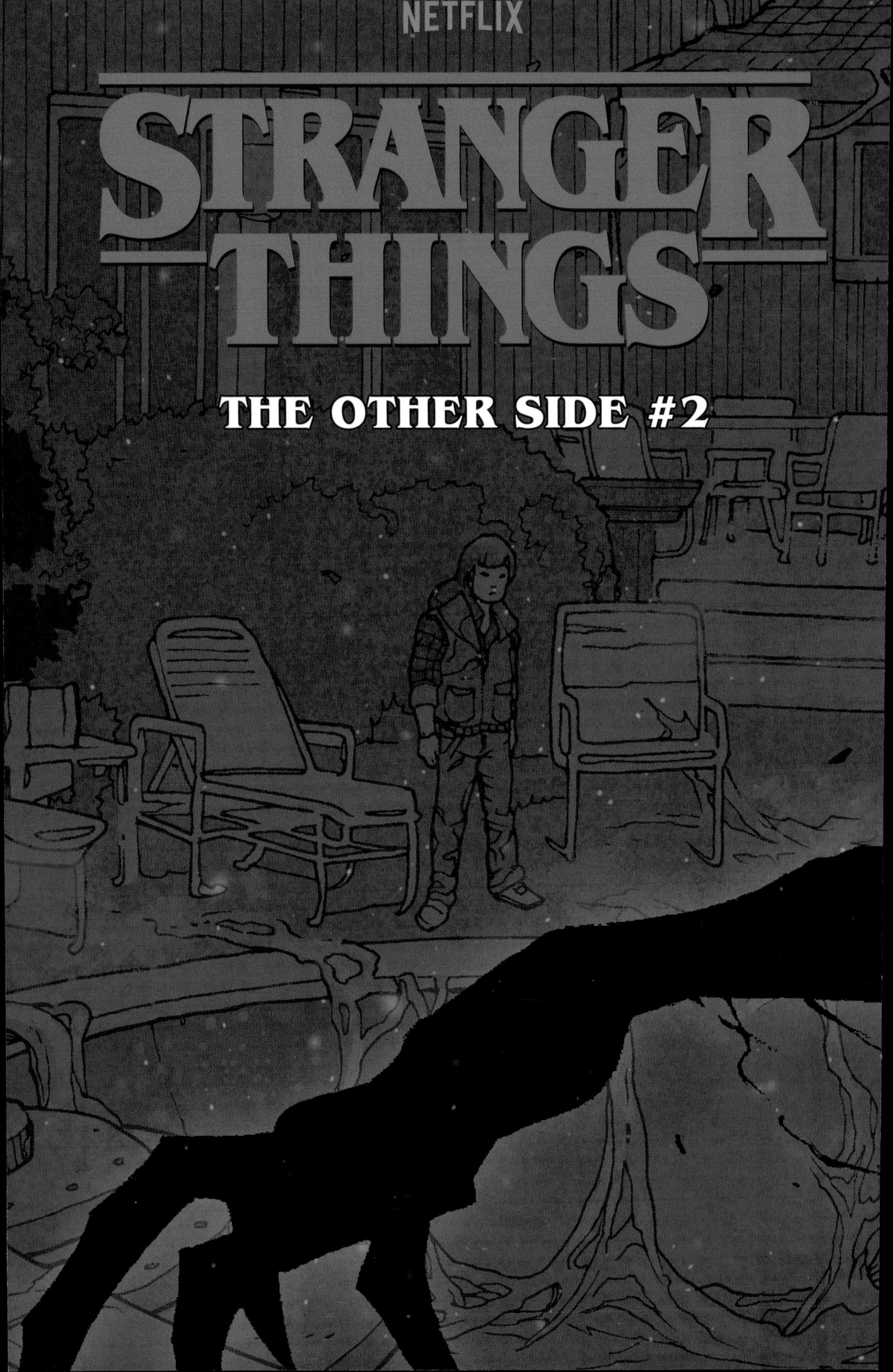
NETFLIX
STRANGER THINGS
THE OTHER SIDE #2

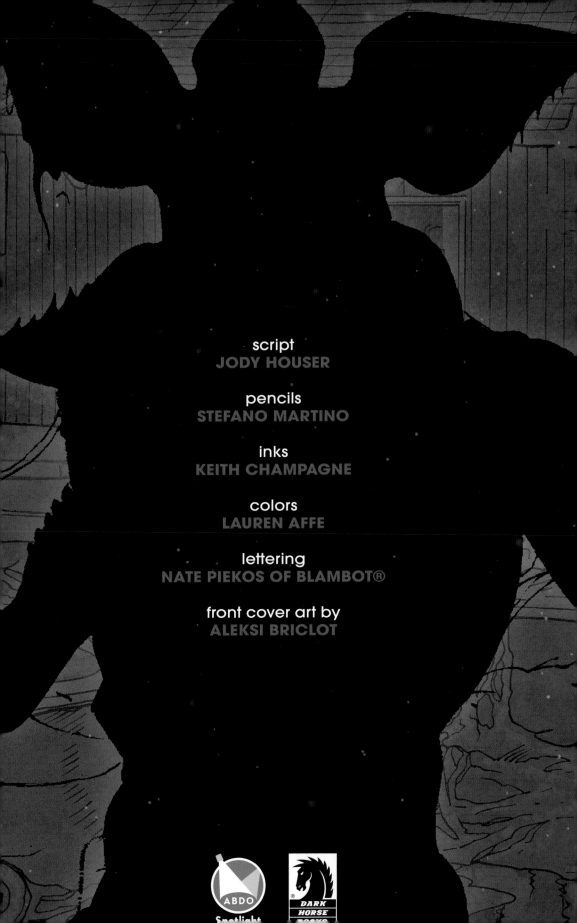

script
JODY HOUSER

pencils
STEFANO MARTINO

inks
KEITH CHAMPAGNE

colors
LAUREN AFFE

lettering
NATE PIEKOS OF BLAMBOT®

front cover art by
ALEKSI BRICLOT

ABDO
Spotlight

DARK
HORSE
BOOKS

ABDOBOOKS.COM

Reinforced library bound edition published in 2020 by Spotlight, a division of ABDO,
PO Box 398166, Minneapolis, Minnesota 55439. Spotlight produces high-quality
reinforced library bound editions for schools and libraries.
Published by agreement with Dark Horse Comics.

Printed in the United States of America, North Mankato, Minnesota.
042019
092019

THIS BOOK CONTAINS
RECYCLED MATERIALS

Stranger Things™ & © 2019 Netflix. All rights reserved. Dark Horse Comics®
and the Dark Horse logo are trademarks of Dark Horse Comics LLC, registered in
various categories and countries. All rights reserved.

Library of Congress Control Number: 2019939089

Publisher's Cataloging-in-Publication Data

Names: Houser, Jody, author. | Martino, Stefano; Champagne, Keith; Affe, Lauren,
    illustrators.
Title: The other side / writer: Jody Houser; art: Stefano Martino; Keith Champagne;
    Lauren Affe.
Description: Minneapolis, Minnesota: Spotlight, 2020 | Series: Stranger things
Summary: This spine-tingling comic based on the hit Netflix series follows Will Byers'
    struggle to survive in the treacherous Upside Down.
Identifiers: ISBN 9781532143878 (#1; lib. bdg.) | ISBN 9781532143885 (#2; lib. bdg.) |
    ISBN 9781532143892 (#3; lib. bdg.) | ISBN 9781532143908 (#4; lib. bdg.)
Subjects: LCSH: Stranger things (Television program)--Juvenile fiction. | Science
    fiction television programs--Juvenile fiction. | Supernatural disappearances--
    Juvenile fiction. | Monsters--Juvenile fiction. | Graphic novels--Juvenile fiction. |
    Comic books, strips, etc.--Juvenile fiction
Classification: DDC 741.5--dc2

Spotlight

A Division of ABDO
abdobooks.com

WILL BYERS IS SO VERY FAR AWAY FROM HOME.

HE'S SURROUNDED BY A DARK MOCKERY OF THE WORLD HE KNOWS.

HAUNTED BY LOVING VOICES THAT REMAIN JUST OUT OF REACH.

WHO-- *SHHK*-- THIS?!

AND SOMEHOW, THE SHADES OF THE FAMILIAR, TWISTED JUST SO...

...MAKES HIM FEEL THAT MUCH MORE LOST.

SSKRRRR

WHAT HAVE--*SHHK*-- DONE TO MY-- *SHHHHHHH*

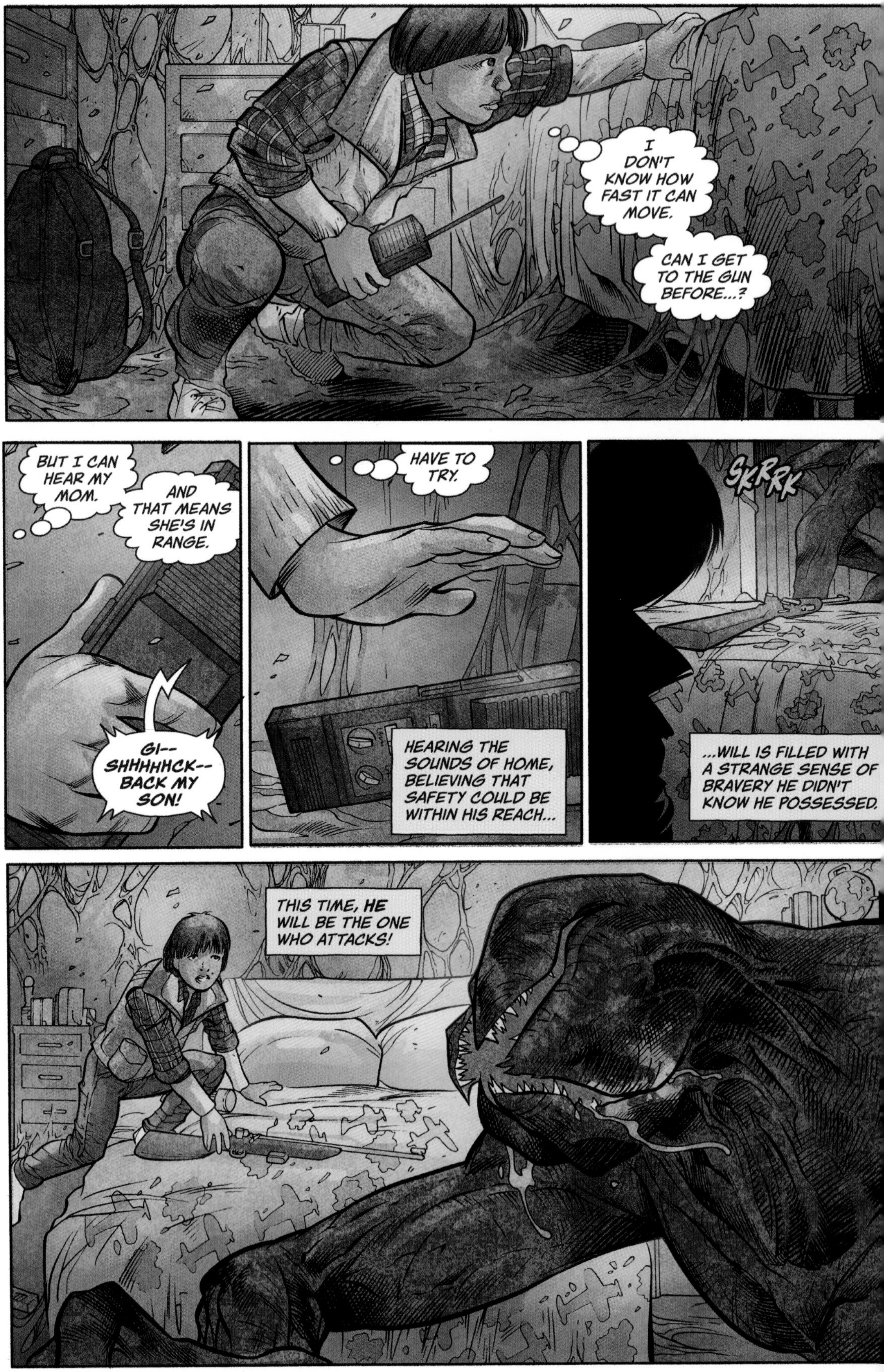
I DON'T KNOW HOW FAST IT CAN MOVE.
CAN I GET TO THE GUN BEFORE...?
BUT I CAN HEAR MY MOM.
AND THAT MEANS SHE'S IN RANGE.
GI-- SHHHHHCK-- BACK MY SON!
HAVE TO TRY.
HEARING THE SOUNDS OF HOME, BELIEVING THAT SAFETY COULD BE WITHIN HIS REACH...
SKRRK
...WILL IS FILLED WITH A STRANGE SENSE OF BRAVERY HE DIDN'T KNOW HE POSSESSED.
THIS TIME, HE WILL BE THE ONE WHO ATTACKS!

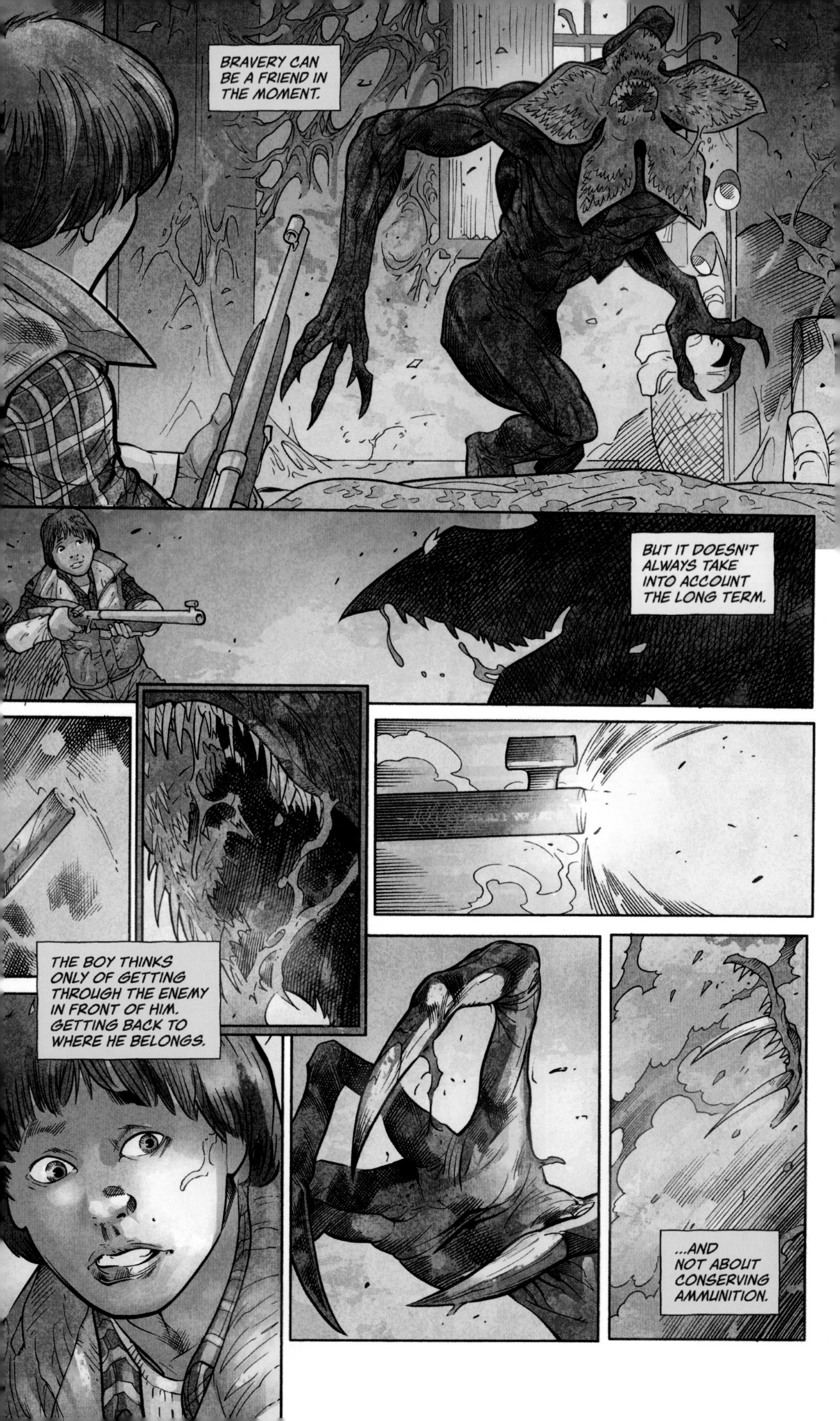

BRAVERY CAN BE A FRIEND IN THE MOMENT.
BUT IT DOESN'T ALWAYS TAKE INTO ACCOUNT THE LONG TERM.
THE BOY THINKS ONLY OF GETTING THROUGH THE ENEMY IN FRONT OF HIM. GETTING BACK TO WHERE HE BELONGS.
...AND NOT ABOUT CONSERVING AMMUNITION.

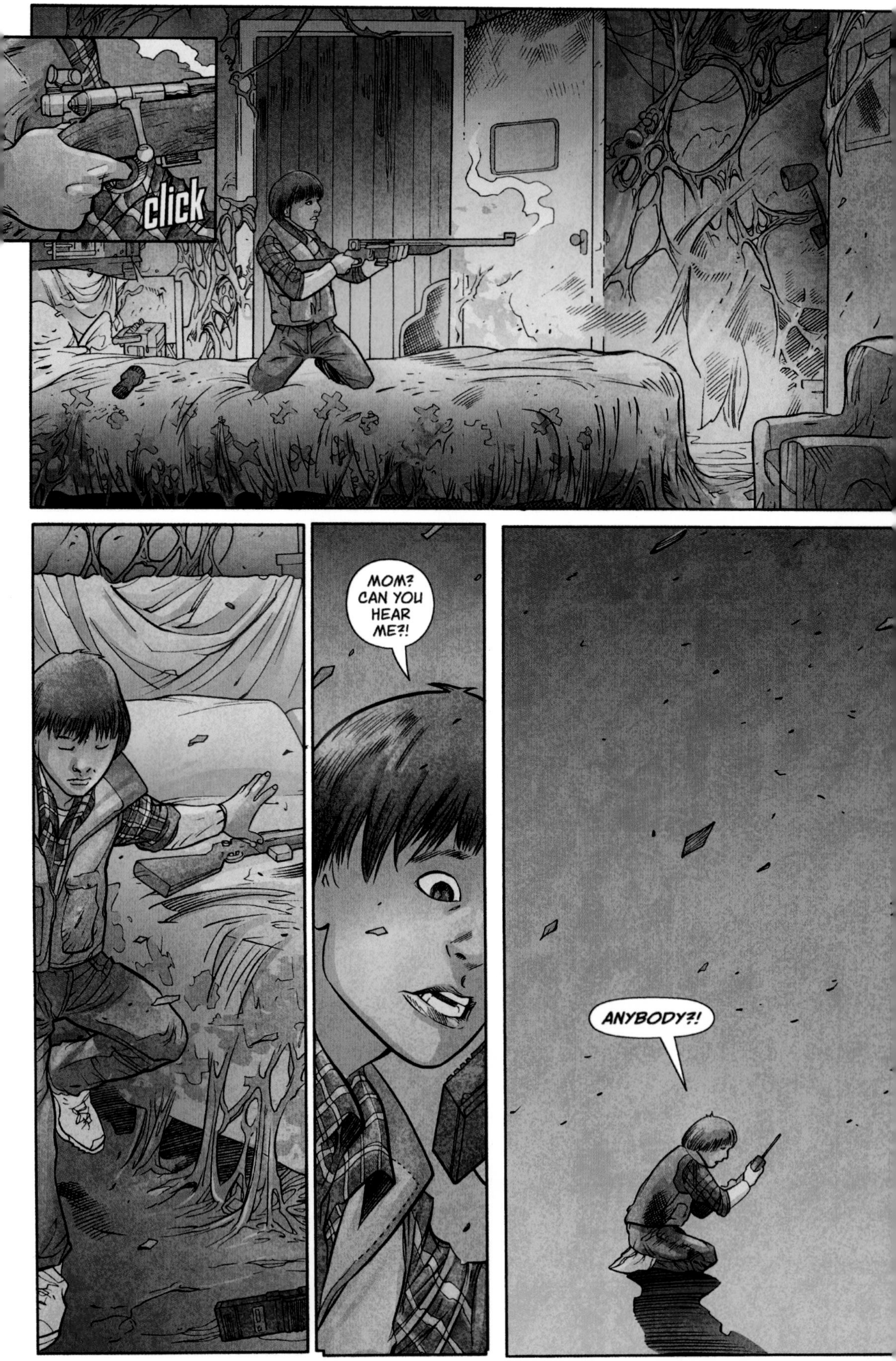
click
MOM? CAN YOU HEAR ME?!
ANYBODY?!

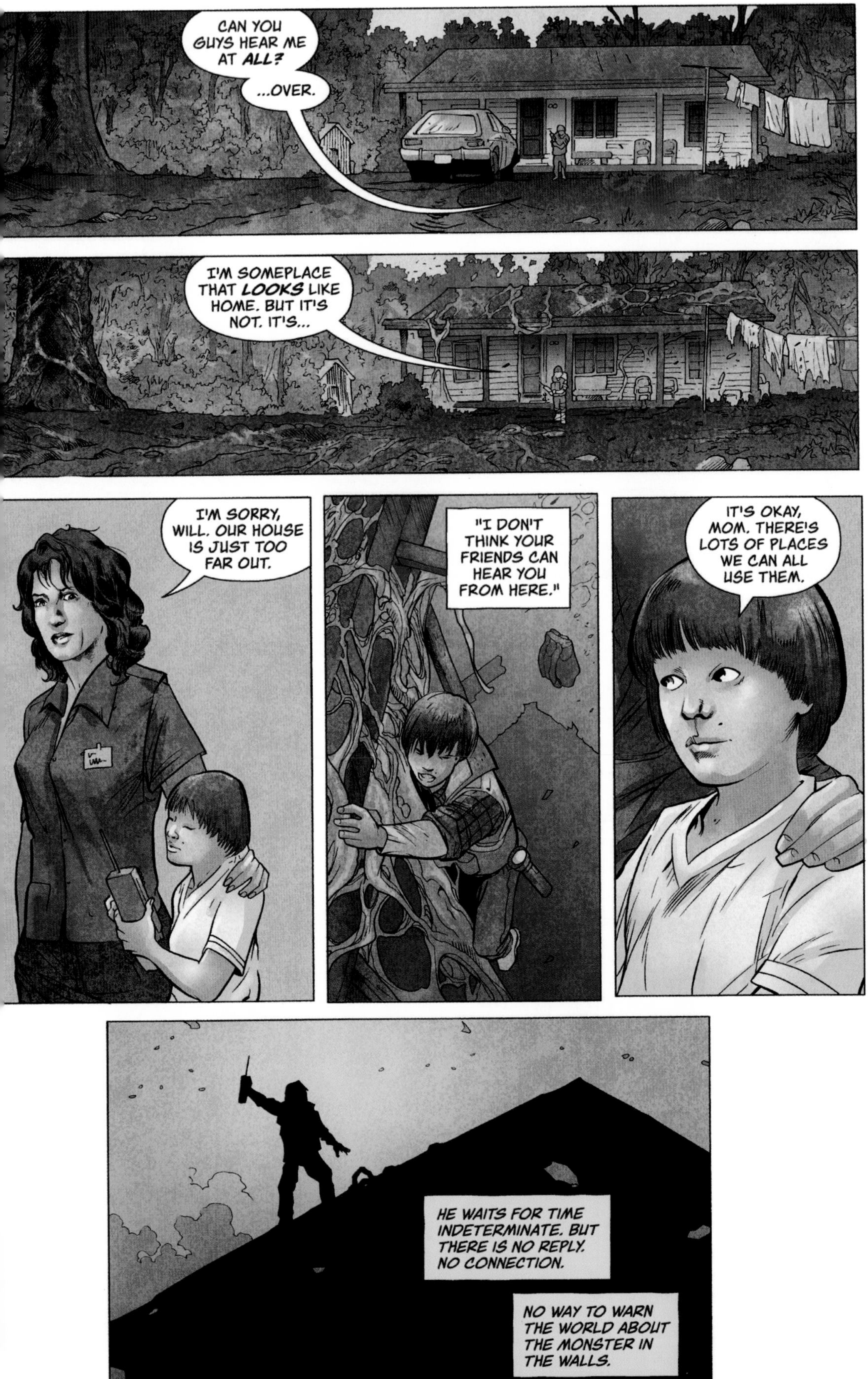
CAN YOU GUYS HEAR ME AT ALL?
...OVER.
I'M SOMEPLACE THAT LOOKS LIKE HOME. BUT IT'S NOT. IT'S...
I'M SORRY, WILL. OUR HOUSE IS JUST TOO FAR OUT.
"I DON'T THINK YOUR FRIENDS CAN HEAR YOU FROM HERE."
IT'S OKAY, MOM. THERE'S LOTS OF PLACES WE CAN ALL USE THEM.
HE WAITS FOR TIME INDETERMINATE. BUT THERE IS NO REPLY. NO CONNECTION.
NO WAY TO WARN THE WORLD ABOUT THE MONSTER IN THE WALLS.

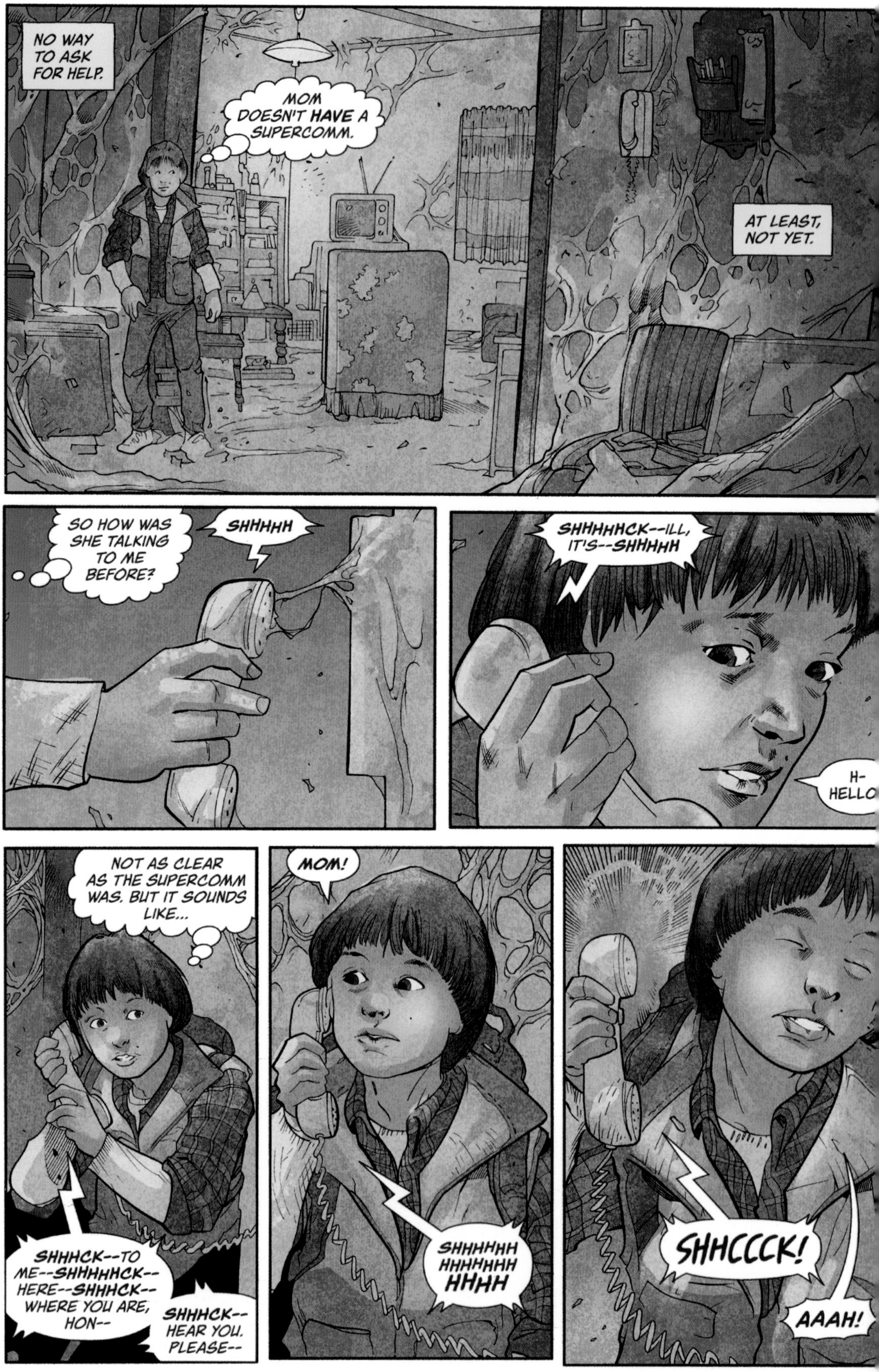
NO WAY TO ASK FOR HELP.
MOM DOESN'T HAVE A SUPERCOMM.
AT LEAST, NOT YET.
SO HOW WAS SHE TALKING TO ME BEFORE?
SHHHHH
SHHHHHCK--ILL, IT'S--SHHHHH
H- HELLO
NOT AS CLEAR AS THE SUPERCOMM WAS. BUT IT SOUNDS LIKE...
SHHHCK--TO ME--SHHHHHCK--HERE--SHHHCK--WHERE YOU ARE, HON--
SHHHCK--HEAR YOU. PLEASE--
MOM!
SHHHHHH HHHHHHH HHHH
SHHCCCK!
AAAH!

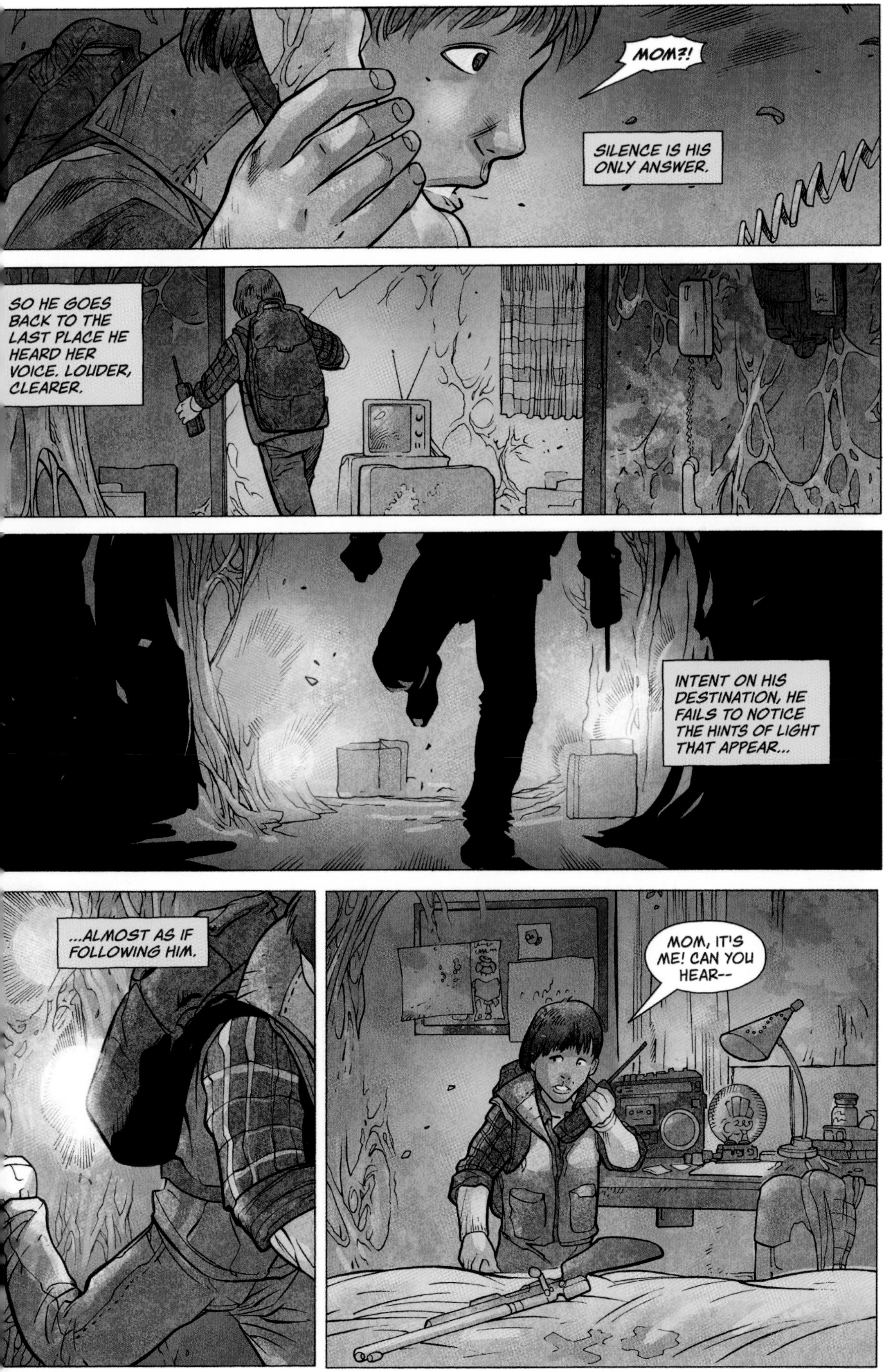
MOM?!
SILENCE IS HIS ONLY ANSWER.
SO HE GOES BACK TO THE LAST PLACE HE HEARD HER VOICE. LOUDER, CLEARER.
INTENT ON HIS DESTINATION, HE FAILS TO NOTICE THE HINTS OF LIGHT THAT APPEAR...
...ALMOST AS IF FOLLOWING HIM.
MOM, IT'S ME! CAN YOU HEAR--

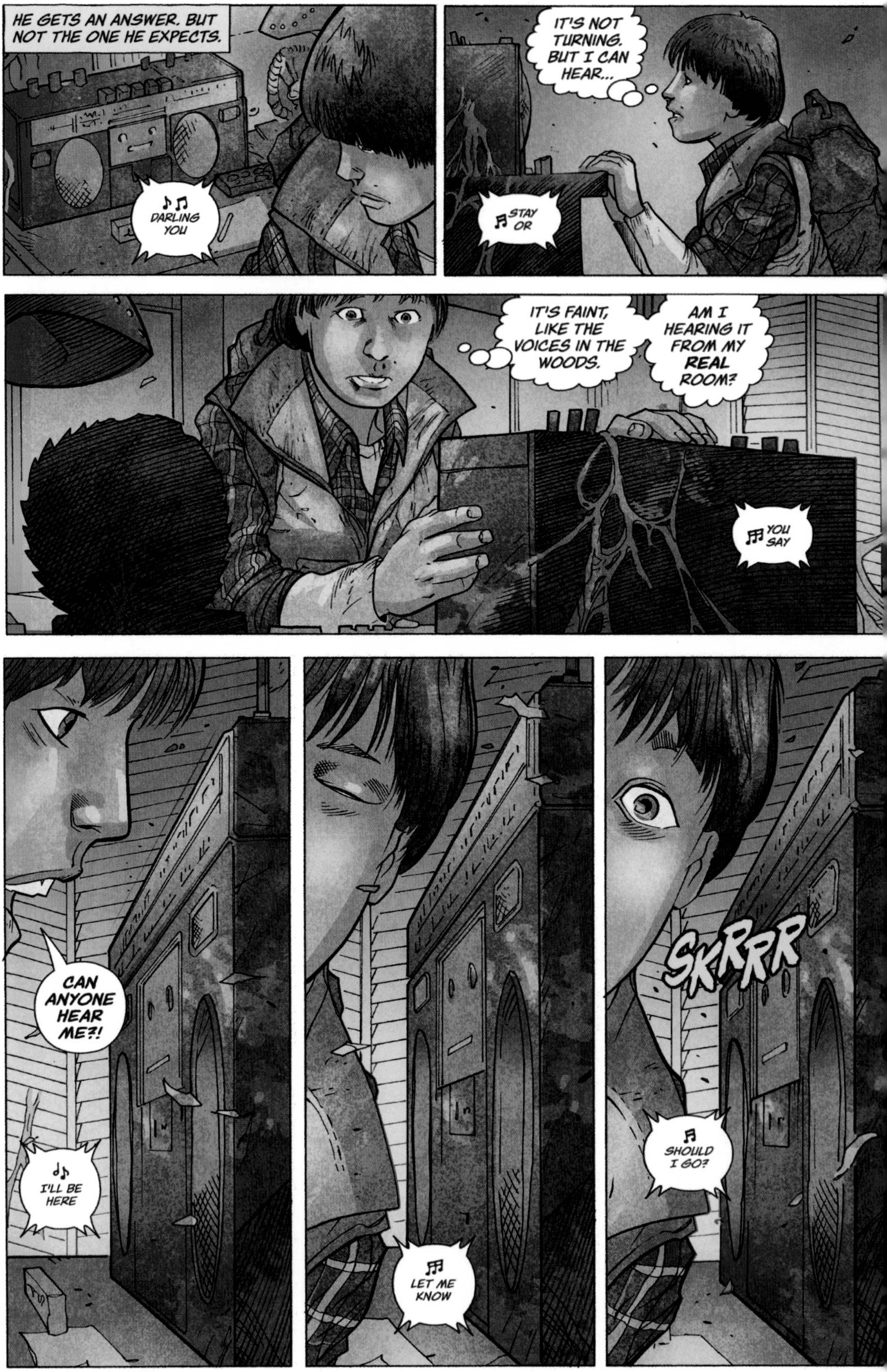
HE GETS AN ANSWER. BUT NOT THE ONE HE EXPECTS.
DARLING YOU
IT'S NOT TURNING. BUT I CAN HEAR...
STAY OR
IT'S FAINT, LIKE THE VOICES IN THE WOODS.
AM I HEARING IT FROM MY REAL ROOM?
YOU SAY
CAN ANYONE HEAR ME?!
I'LL BE HERE
LET ME KNOW
SKRRR
SHOULD I GO?

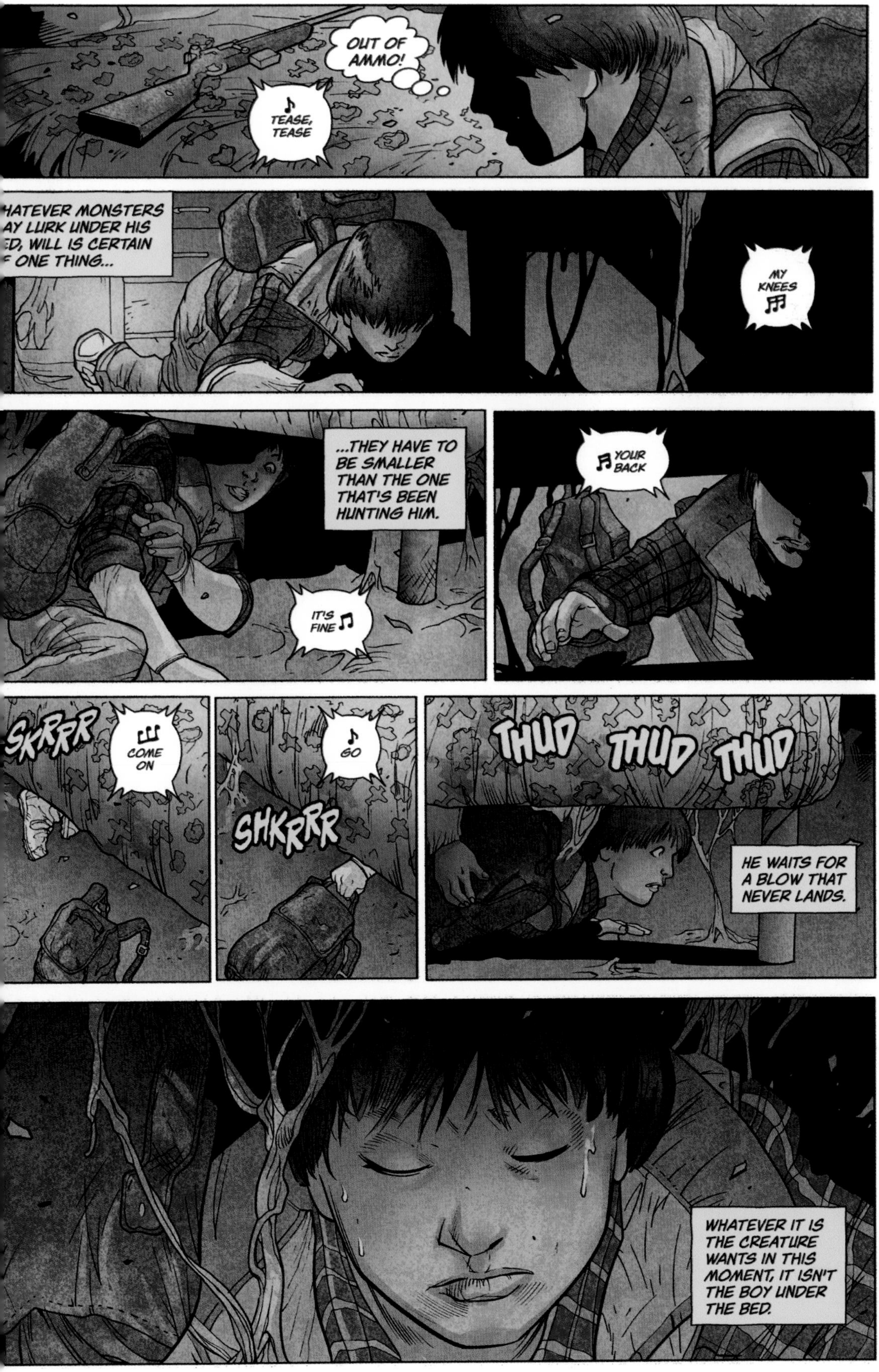
OUT OF AMMO!
♪ TEASE, TEASE
HATEVER MONSTERS AY LURK UNDER HIS ED, WILL IS CERTAIN F ONE THING...
MY KNEES ♫
...THEY HAVE TO BE SMALLER THAN THE ONE THAT'S BEEN HUNTING HIM.
IT'S FINE ♫
♫ YOUR BACK
SKRRR
COME ON
♪ GO
SHKRRR
THUD THUD THUD
HE WAITS FOR A BLOW THAT NEVER LANDS.
WHATEVER IT IS THE CREATURE WANTS IN THIS MOMENT, IT ISN'T THE BOY UNDER THE BED.

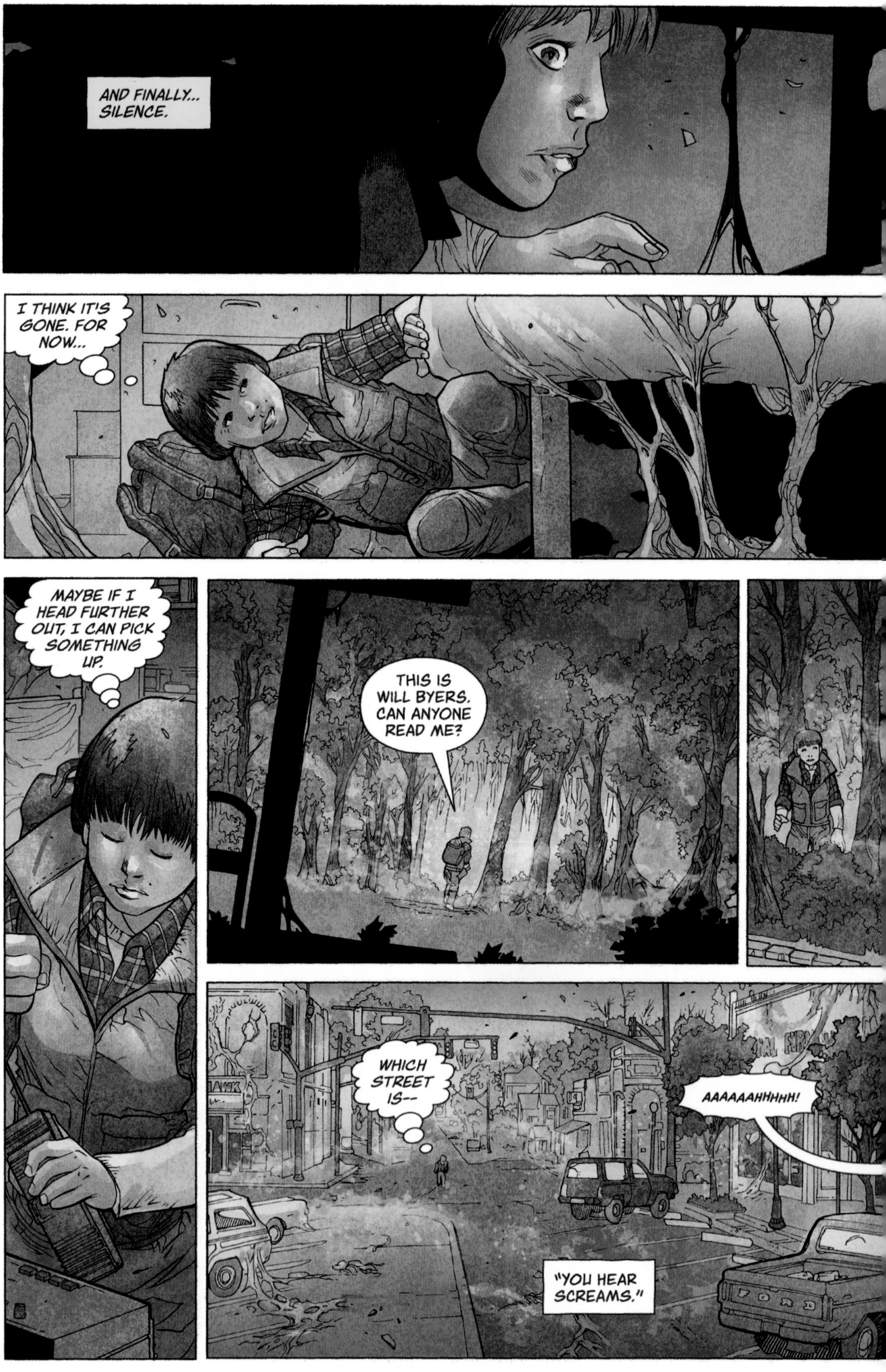

AND FINALLY... SILENCE.
I THINK IT'S GONE. FOR NOW...
MAYBE IF I HEAD FURTHER OUT, I CAN PICK SOMETHING UP.
THIS IS WILL BYERS. CAN ANYONE READ ME?
WHICH STREET IS--
AAAAAAHHHHH!
"YOU HEAR SCREAMS."

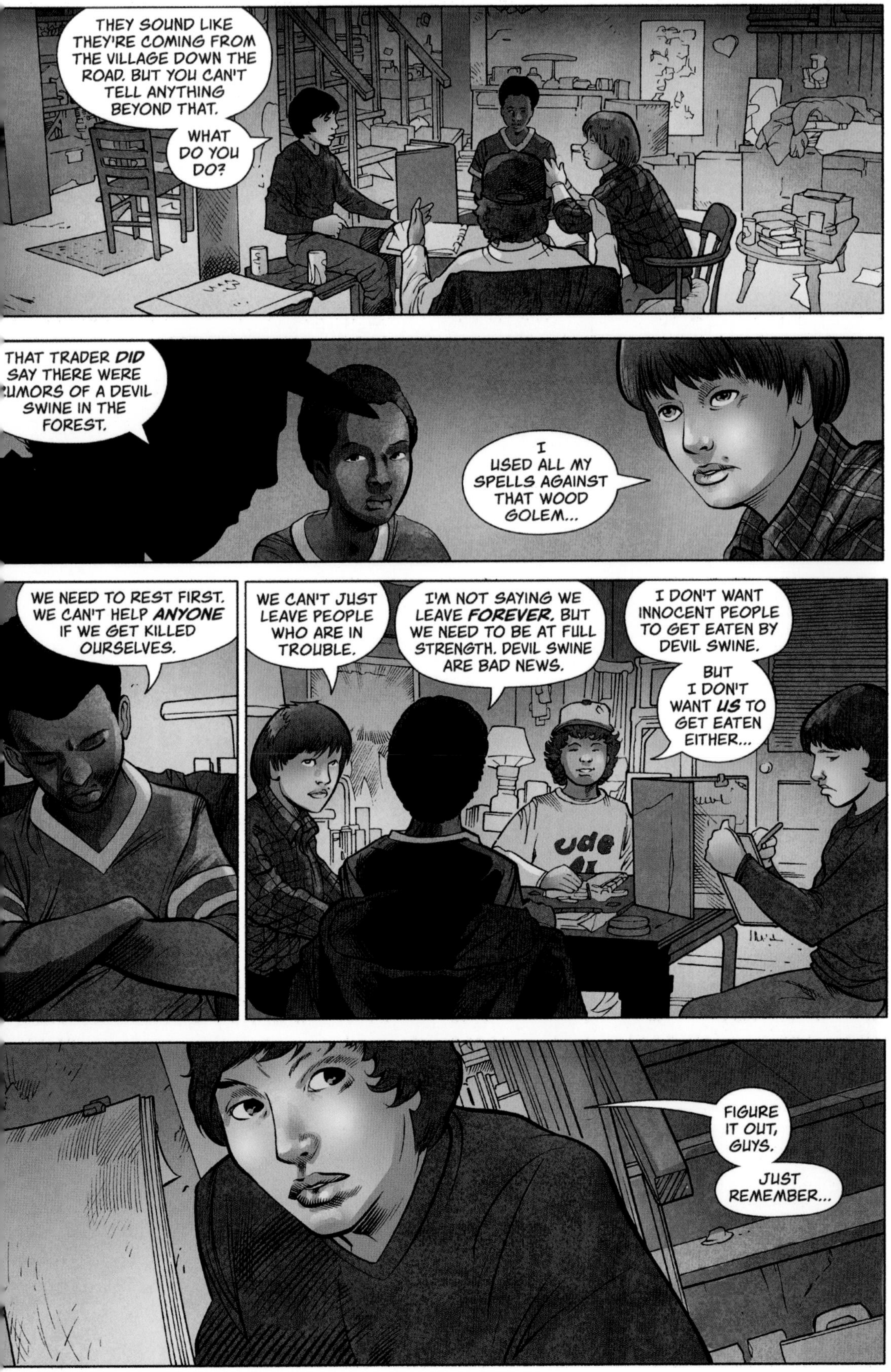
THEY SOUND LIKE THEY'RE COMING FROM THE VILLAGE DOWN THE ROAD. BUT YOU CAN'T TELL ANYTHING BEYOND THAT.
WHAT DO YOU DO?
THAT TRADER DID SAY THERE WERE RUMORS OF A DEVIL SWINE IN THE FOREST.
I USED ALL MY SPELLS AGAINST THAT WOOD GOLEM...
WE NEED TO REST FIRST. WE CAN'T HELP ANYONE IF WE GET KILLED OURSELVES.
WE CAN'T JUST LEAVE PEOPLE WHO ARE IN TROUBLE.
I'M NOT SAYING WE LEAVE FOREVER. BUT WE NEED TO BE AT FULL STRENGTH. DEVIL SWINE ARE BAD NEWS.
I DON'T WANT INNOCENT PEOPLE TO GET EATEN BY DEVIL SWINE.
BUT I DON'T WANT US TO GET EATEN EITHER...
FIGURE IT OUT, GUYS.
JUST REMEMBER...

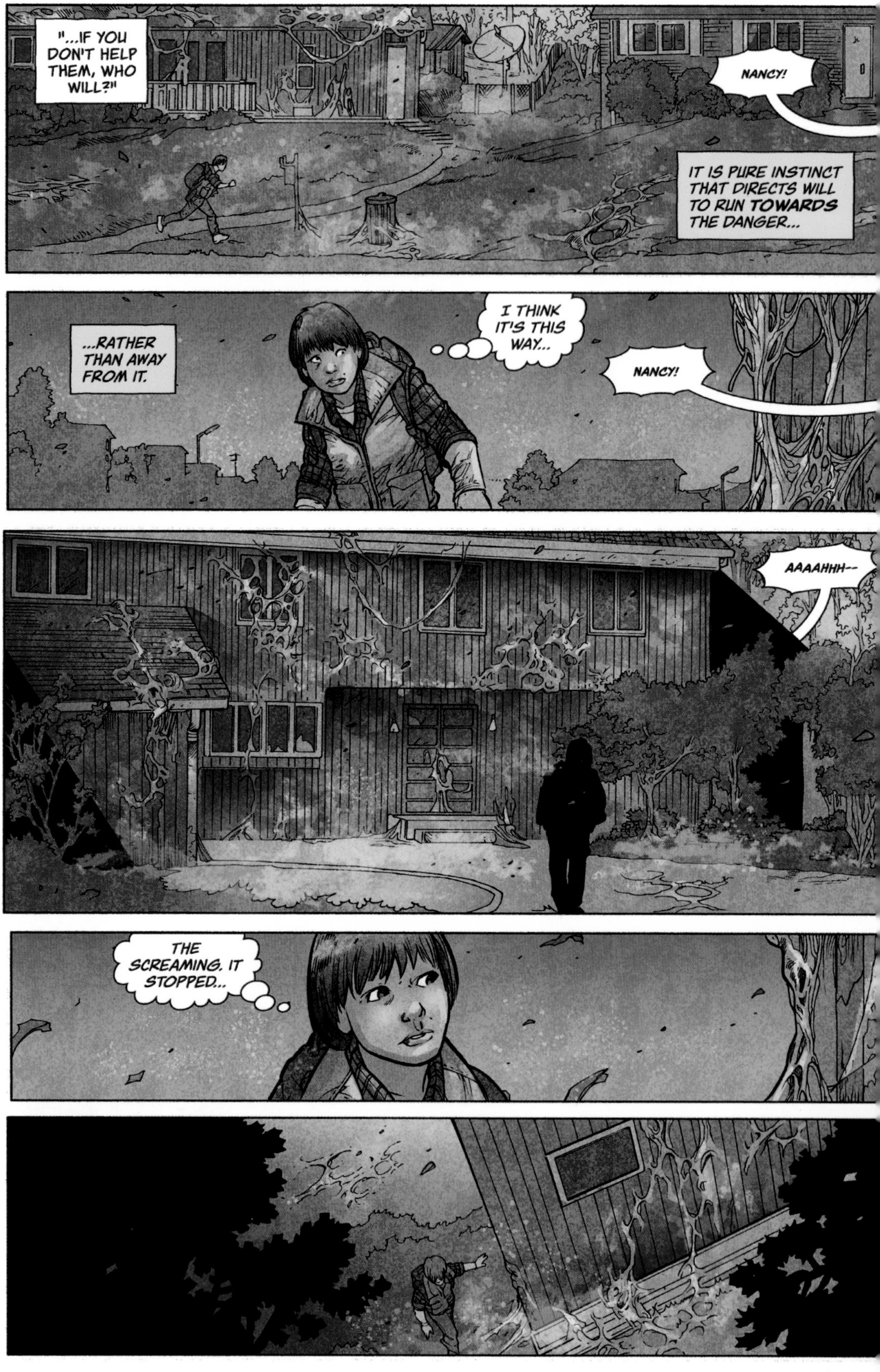
"...IF YOU DON'T HELP THEM, WHO WILL?"
NANCY!
IT IS PURE INSTINCT THAT DIRECTS WILL TO RUN **TOWARDS** THE DANGER...
...RATHER THAN AWAY FROM IT.
I THINK IT'S THIS WAY...
NANCY!
AAAAHHH--
THE SCREAMING. IT STOPPED...

HELLO? IS ANYONE--

ARE THESE FROM THE GIRL WHO SCREAMED?

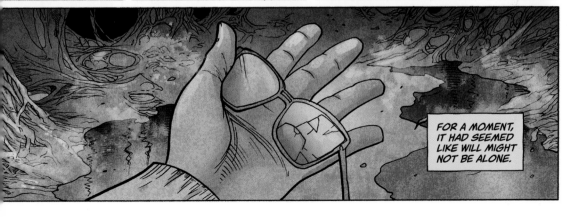

FOR A MOMENT, IT HAD SEEMED LIKE WILL MIGHT NOT BE ALONE.

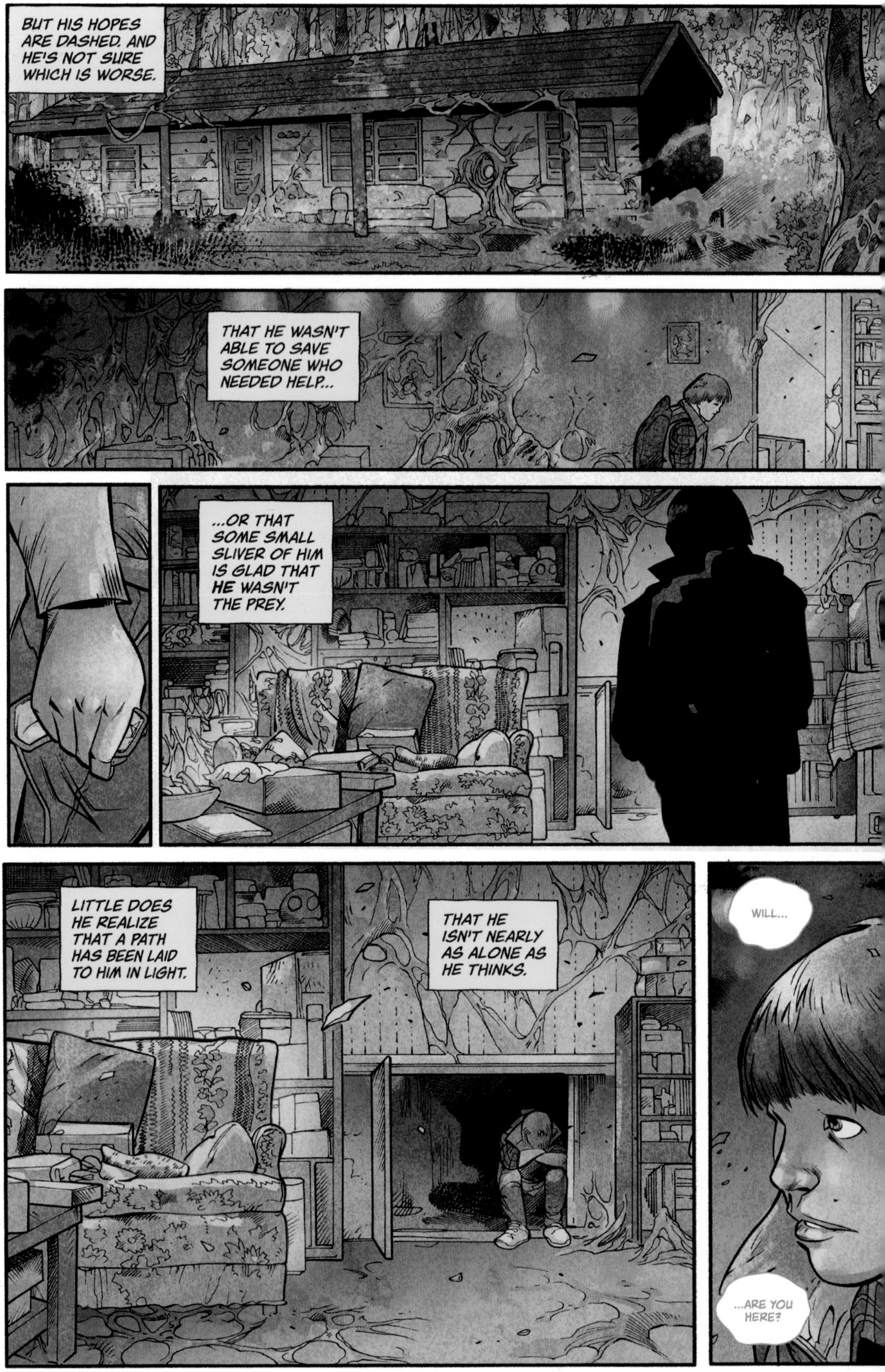
BUT HIS HOPES ARE DASHED. AND HE'S NOT SURE WHICH IS WORSE.
THAT HE WASN'T ABLE TO SAVE SOMEONE WHO NEEDED HELP...
...OR THAT SOME SMALL SLIVER OF HIM IS GLAD THAT **HE** WASN'T THE PREY.
LITTLE DOES HE REALIZE THAT A PATH HAS BEEN LAID TO HIM IN LIGHT.
THAT HE ISN'T NEARLY AS ALONE AS HE THINKS.
WILL...
...ARE YOU HERE?

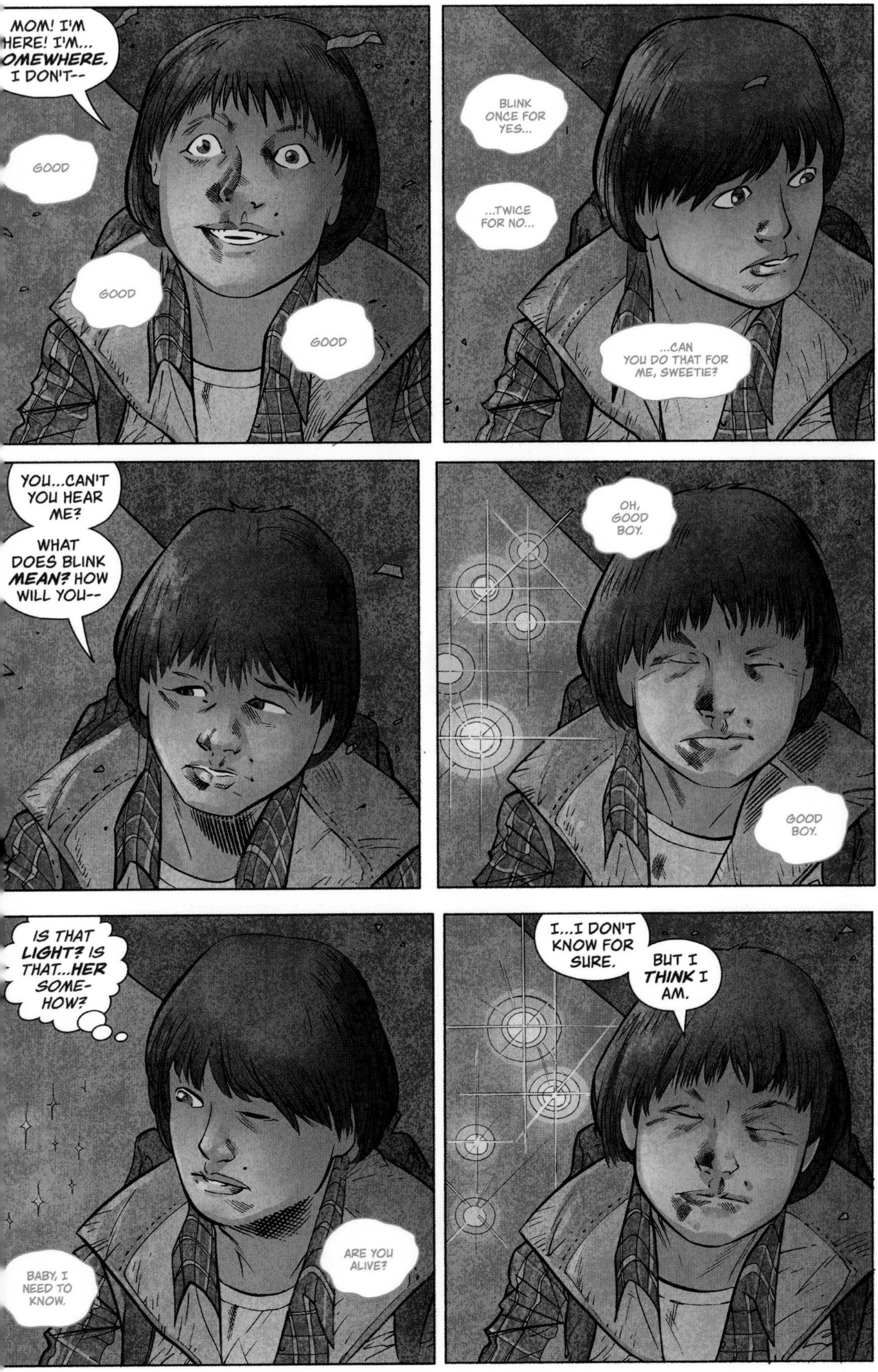

MOM! I'M HERE! I'M... OMEWHERE. I DON'T--
GOOD
GOOD
GOOD
BLINK ONCE FOR YES...
...TWICE FOR NO...
...CAN YOU DO THAT FOR ME, SWEETIE?
YOU...CAN'T YOU HEAR ME?
WHAT DOES BLINK MEAN? HOW WILL YOU--
OH, GOOD BOY.
GOOD BOY.
IS THAT LIGHT? IS THAT...HER SOME-HOW?
BABY, I NEED TO KNOW.
ARE YOU ALIVE?
I...I DON'T KNOW FOR SURE.
BUT I THINK I AM.

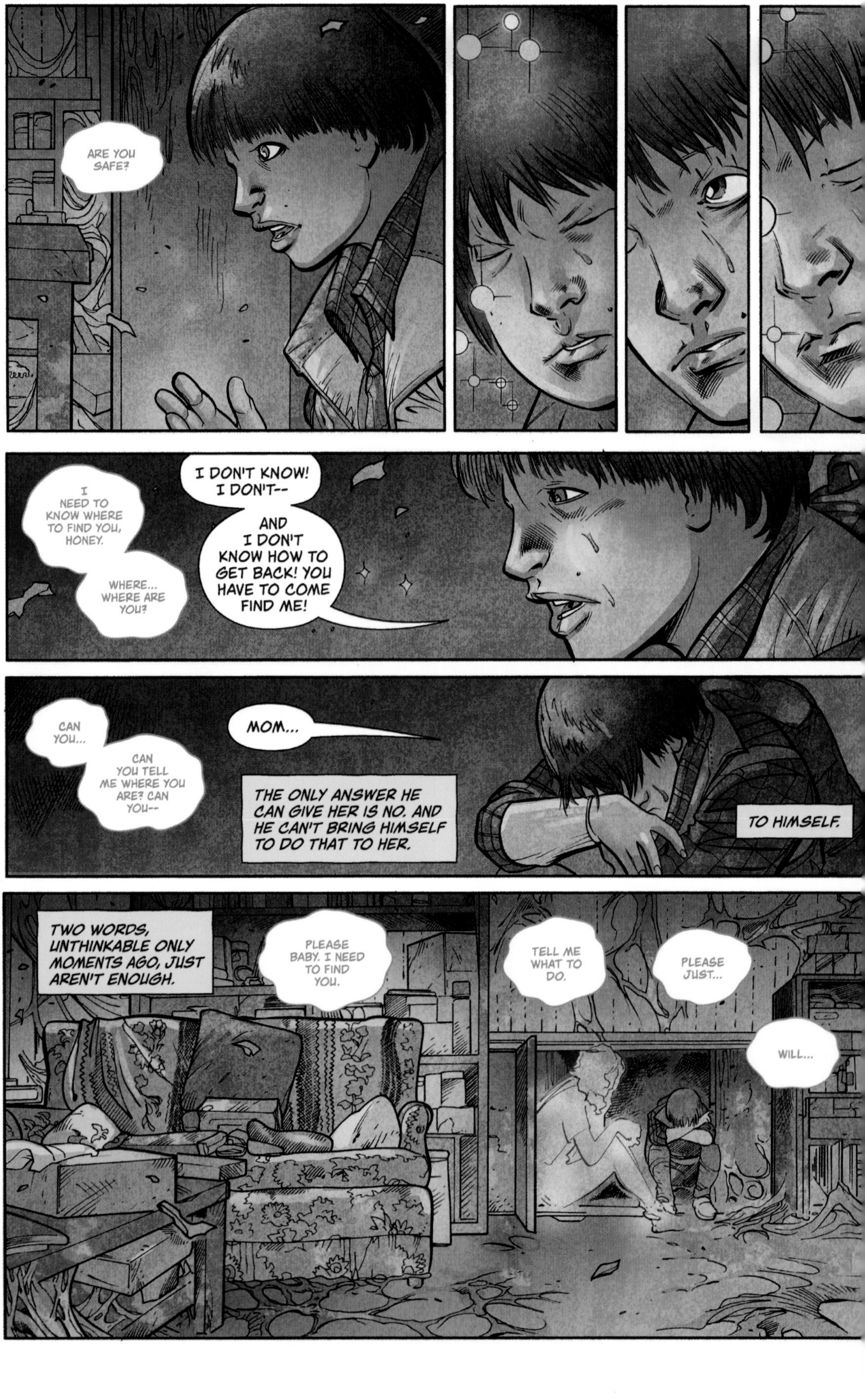
ARE YOU SAFE?
I NEED TO KNOW WHERE TO FIND YOU, HONEY.
I DON'T KNOW! I DON'T--
WHERE... WHERE ARE YOU?
AND I DON'T KNOW HOW TO GET BACK! YOU HAVE TO COME FIND ME!
CAN YOU...
CAN YOU TELL ME WHERE YOU ARE? CAN YOU--
MOM...
THE ONLY ANSWER HE CAN GIVE HER IS NO. AND HE CAN'T BRING HIMSELF TO DO THAT TO HER.
TO HIMSELF.
TWO WORDS, UNTHINKABLE ONLY MOMENTS AGO, JUST AREN'T ENOUGH.
PLEASE BABY. I NEED TO FIND YOU.
TELL ME WHAT TO DO.
PLEASE JUST...
WILL...

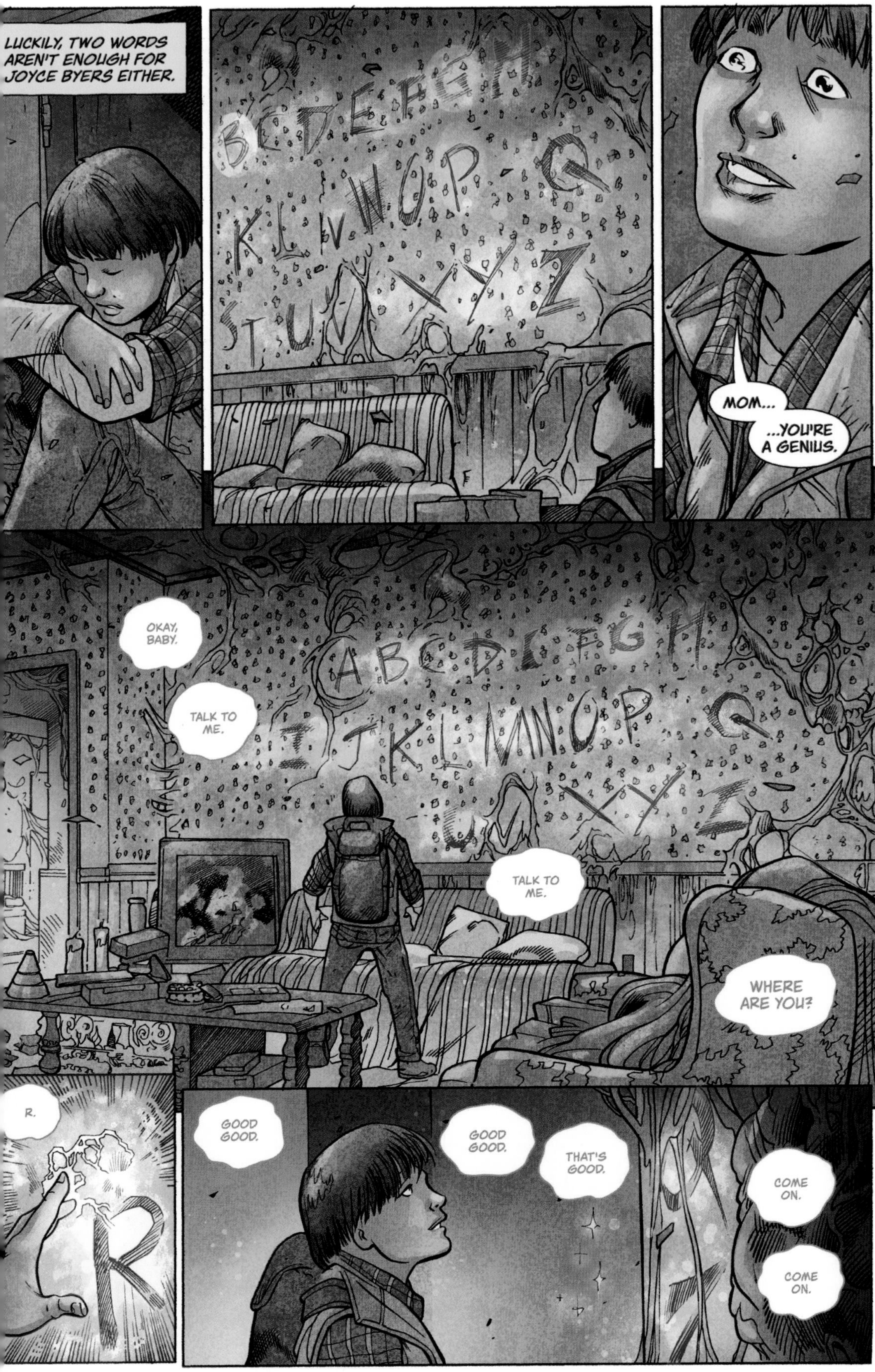
LUCKILY, TWO WORDS AREN'T ENOUGH FOR JOYCE BYERS EITHER.
MOM...
...YOU'RE A GENIUS.
OKAY, BABY.
TALK TO ME.
TALK TO ME.
WHERE ARE YOU?
R.
GOOD GOOD.
GOOD GOOD.
THAT'S GOOD.
COME ON.
COME ON.

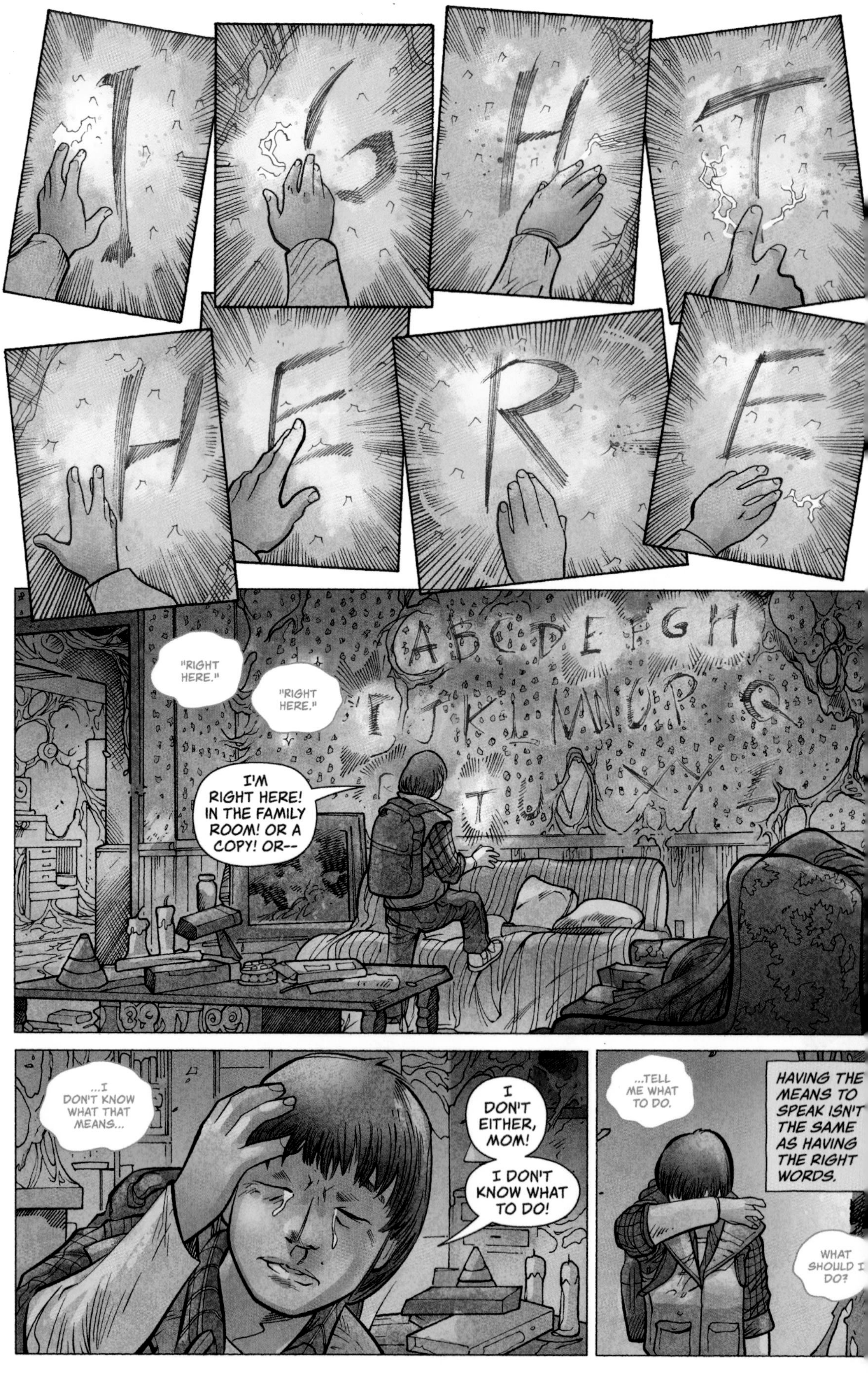
I
G
H
T
H
E
R
E
A B C D E F G H
I J K L M N O P Q
T U V W X Y Z
"RIGHT HERE."
"RIGHT HERE."
I'M RIGHT HERE! IN THE FAMILY ROOM! OR A COPY! OR--
...I DON'T KNOW WHAT THAT MEANS...
I DON'T EITHER, MOM!
I DON'T KNOW WHAT TO DO!
...TELL ME WHAT TO DO.
HAVING THE MEANS TO SPEAK ISN'T THE SAME AS HAVING THE RIGHT WORDS.
WHAT SHOULD I DO?

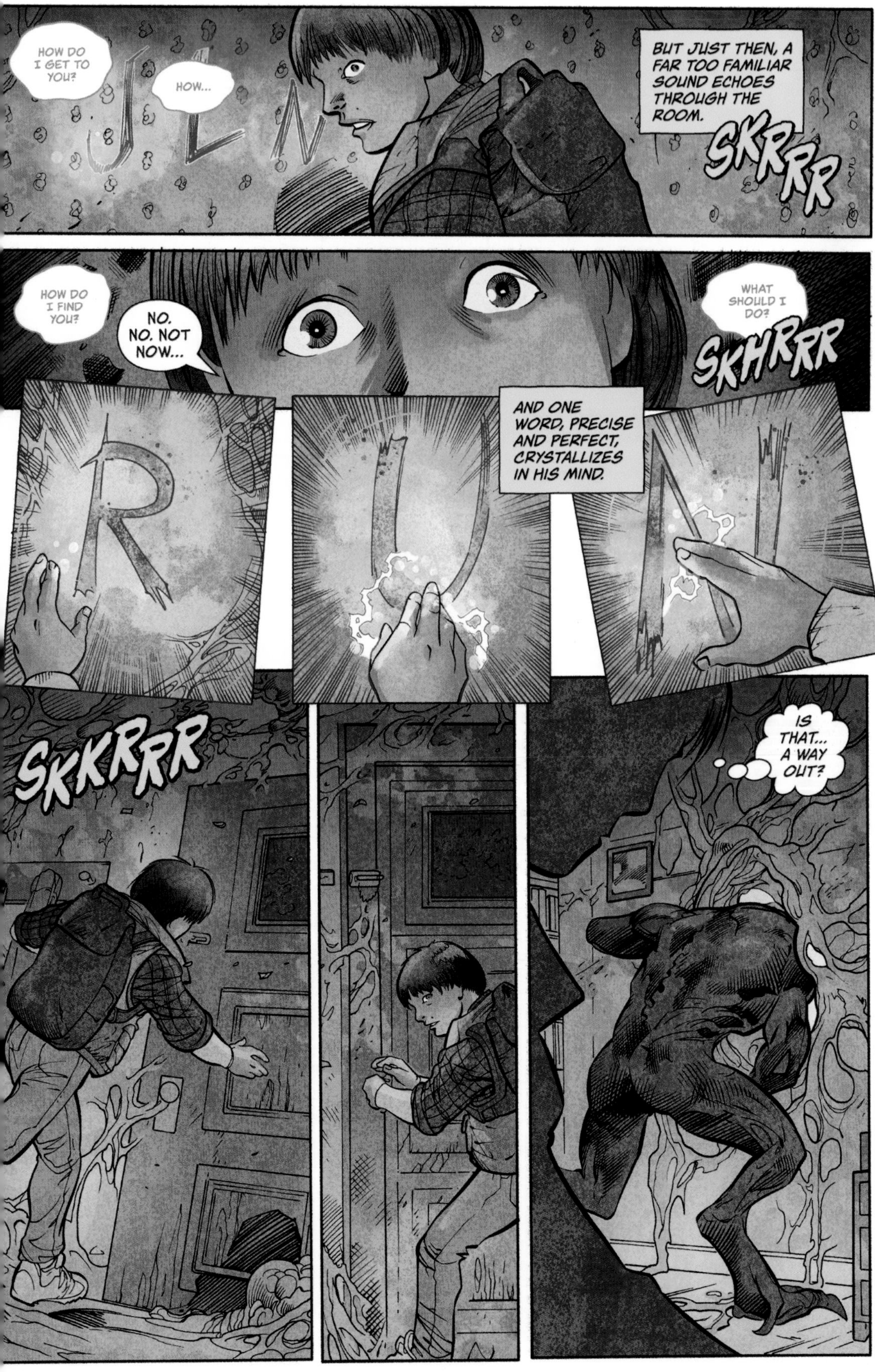
HOW DO I GET TO YOU?
HOW...
BUT JUST THEN, A FAR TOO FAMILIAR SOUND ECHOES THROUGH THE ROOM.
SKRRRR
HOW DO I FIND YOU?
NO. NO. NOT NOW...
WHAT SHOULD I DO?
SKHRRRR
AND ONE WORD, PRECISE AND PERFECT, CRYSTALLIZES IN HIS MIND.
SKKRRRR
IS THAT... A WAY OUT?

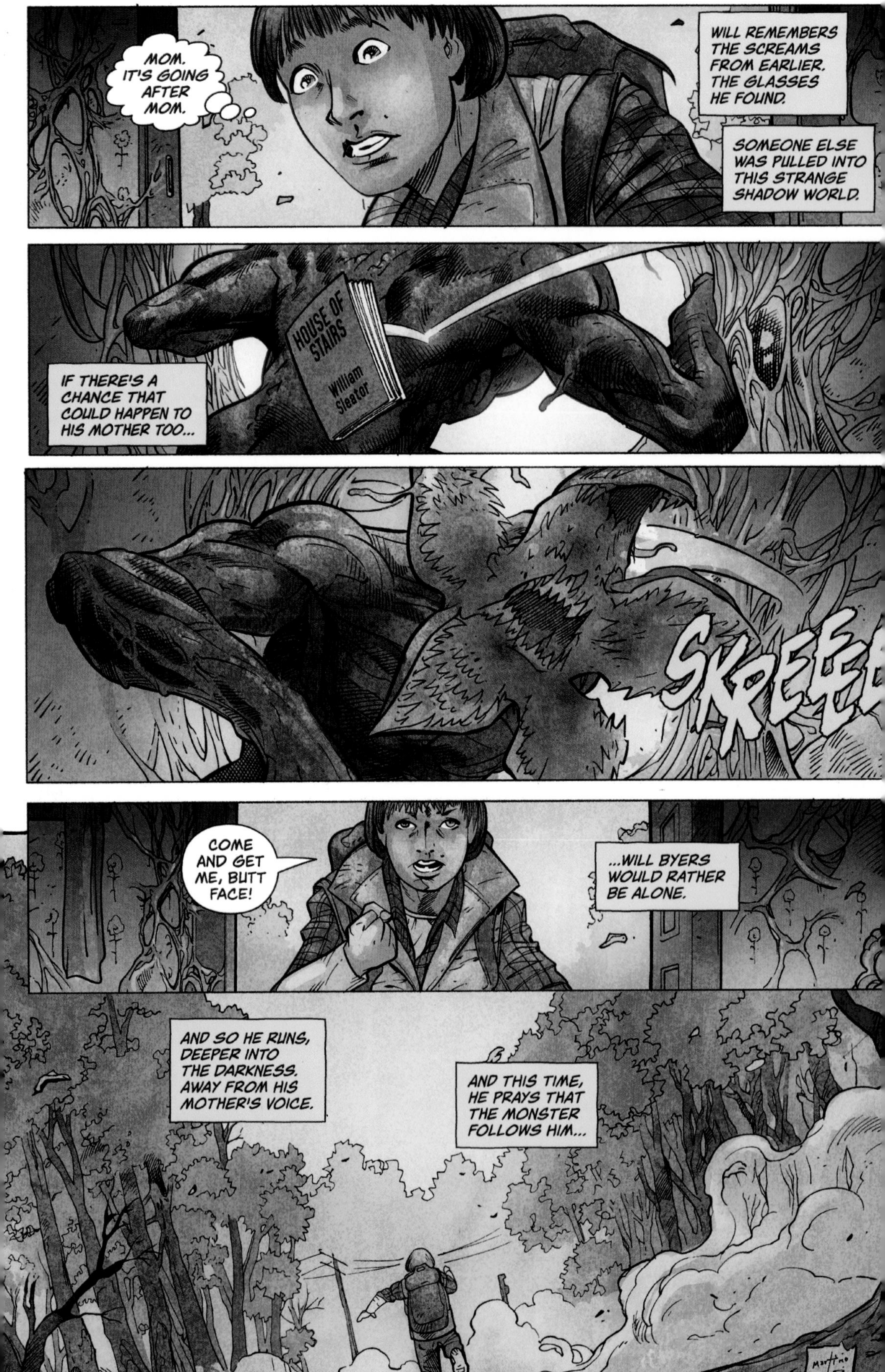
MOM. IT'S GOING AFTER MOM.
WILL REMEMBERS THE SCREAMS FROM EARLIER. THE GLASSES HE FOUND.
SOMEONE ELSE WAS PULLED INTO THIS STRANGE SHADOW WORLD.
HOUSE OF STAIRS William Sleator
IF THERE'S A CHANCE THAT COULD HAPPEN TO HIS MOTHER TOO...
SKREEE
COME AND GET ME, BUTT FACE!
...WILL BYERS WOULD RATHER BE ALONE.
AND SO HE RUNS, DEEPER INTO THE DARKNESS. AWAY FROM HIS MOTHER'S VOICE.
AND THIS TIME, HE PRAYS THAT THE MONSTER FOLLOWS HIM...
TO BE CONTINUED!